A Smile To Brightness

Arpit Taneja

BlueRose ONE.com
Stories Matter

First Published in March 2022

ISBN: 978-93-5611-530-9

BLUEROSE PUBLISHERS

www.BlueRoseONE.com

info@bluerosepublishers.com

+91 8882 898 898

Cover Design:

Geetika

Typographic Design:

Namrata Saini

Distributed by: BlueRose, Amazon, Flipkart

Prologue

1st January 2021

Hearing the sound of crackers as a welcoming ritual for the new year, sitting on the adjoining balcony of my room thinking about just one person, one smile, having a smoke, smiling with teary eyes remembering the days with her, the talks {late night}

Aarohi, the love of my life…

The way it started, the way it concluded makes me cry, but with a smile…

It was in the month of July 2015, when I left my hometown to achieve my dreams.

Residing in Gurgaon, that night {the night} changed me as a person and my whole life…

A story started with a social media profile…

'Contents

Introduction

July 2015

11:05, I was sitting outside my pg room, on my bean bag, weather was surprisingly cold for the month of July, lighting up a cigarette... well, you all will be thinking who is this, my bad.... I apologize...

My name is dhruv arora

I belong to the small town of Ganganagar in Rajasthan.

My family consists of a father, a mother, and an elder sister...

In may I completed my 1st year of graduation in BBA from Bihani College affiliated under Maharaja Ganga Singh University, Ganganagar, and then decided to pursue my dream of becoming a cricketer [which every second child in India dreams of] and I chose Gurgaon for that....

I am an introverted guy who never remained away from his family before, especially his father…

Back to May 2015,

Lighting up a cigarette while sitting in the lobby outside my room was a new hobby i nurtured in the last few days… It has been 3 weeks since I have been away from home… it was decided that i have 2 years to pursue my dreams till my college graduation. If I made a significant improvement or achievement, I will be allowed to continue …

When I came to Gurgaon, I stayed with one of my cousins but then I shifted to a PG which was near to the academy…

It's been a week at the PG and my daily routine consisted of working out, having a talk with my family at 9 at night, and then having cigarettes sitting outside my room…

That day was a little different as I was missing my home, my parents, so the count of cigarettes was on the higher side. Although it was a mandatory routine that we will have a telephonic conversation at 9 at night but that day I was missing them a lot …

Scrolling through different social sites, messaging apps just to confirm that the number of friends I had were fewer than I thought and I won't blame them as after 12th standard one of my girlfriends passed away due to cancer, and for a year I acted differently and as time passed people started forgetting me…

At that time Facebook was hit amongst our generation… the preferred app for bragging, showing off, and complaining about their life…

So, I started scrolling through my news feed, looking for something that might cheer up my mood…

After finding nothing, I lit up a cigarette and decided to see 'the people you may know' bar….

Scrolling through it one profile caught my attention…

A girl profile named Aarohi. I clicked on the profile picture of a girl with a face tilted a little upright [kind of a selfie] she was wearing a pink top, mischievous round eyes, a smile to brighten up a dull day. Silky hair, around, and cute face.

Then I decided to see her 'About' section as soon as I opened it… 'What the fuck' was my instant reaction.

Studied at Bihani college, Ganganagar.

And I was like, she is studying in the same college, how the fuck can I miss this face being in the same college, then reality struck me hard, I didn't even attend a single class or i would say a single day of college in my first year…

"She is cute" was the only thing I said and shut the app.

And decided to have some sleep….

Our first instance

After the last smoke for the day, I went into the room, placed the bean bag in such a manner that it won't trouble, my roommate, neither in the morning nor in the night, if he woke up for a nature call in the middle of the night. I sat on my bed for a little while and I thought 'put off the alarms so that it won't disturb my roommate's sleep as I have to wake up around 5 to for cricket practice session…'.

After a few minutes of trying hard, restlessness was creeping into my mind. I was occupied with one thought, I have no one to share things like my happiness, mood swings, my time etc …. And to add to my restless night was this profile which I saw a few moments ago…

And when you are addicted to smoking, you look at cigarettes as a solution to every problem, issues, and mood, but unfortunately that day, I ran out of cigarettes sticks, so I went to a nearby store that was around 500m away from my PG [a shop near the bus stand] it was late night and that was the only shop I was sure of being open at this hour... I bought a packet of Marlboro advance and was sitting outside my room when I opened Facebook again...

Search bar

'Aarohi'

Opened profile.

Went through her friend list. Found lots of mutuals, some I liked, some I didn't... went through her posts, got confused about what to do and what not to do.

Shutting app.

Opening it.

Repeat.

Thinking...

After some time.

Aarohi

Send friend request

Sent...

Turned off the app.

Picked my bean bag.

Entered my room.

Dozed off.

At 5:00 am my phone alarm went off and the peaceful sleep of mine got compromised. It was an unpleasant surprise and I started searching for that voice bomb which I call my mobile hastily and then turned it off. The late-night fiasco made me forget to turn off the alarm before sleeping. checking my roommate whether my silly mistake has cost him his sleep or I was quick enough to turn off my voice bomb [mobile] but seeing him sleep I took a sigh of relief and switched off my phone and went to take a shower.

[The day I joined the academy, the first resolution I took is to never carry an android phone to the academy with me as I didn't want my focus to be sacrificed or disturbed at any cost…]

After having a shower, I got ready for the academy without making any more noise, I picked up my mp3 player and Samsung guru [the keypad phone which can only be used for text or call which I carry to the academy] in case of some emergency… picked up my bike key… and after having a coffee at PG canteen...,

I reached the academy…

11: oo am: The time for our practice session to conclude… I went straight to PG canteen. After having four boiled eggs as a pre-workout meal, I hit the gym running.

[My gym was 2 kmaway from my PG]

1:00 pm: After the workout, I came back to my room before stopping at the canteen and ordered some lunch. I was feeling more tired that day due to lack of sleep last night, but not for one second did the last night fiasco, occurrence, situation struck my mind…

After having a satisfactory lunch, I was about to doze off when I decided to turn on my android...

Display came back to life from darkness, the notification started making a whistling sound...

I was about to turn the phone into silent mode.... When the notification bar brought a surprise for me...

New notification: Facebook

Aarohi has accepted your friend request.

Late-night fiasco, situation, occurrence, restlessness just came calling my name and knocking my head.

I picked up my phone opened the app and checked it twice "Is it for real?".

And to my surprise "Yes, it was real".

Then my mind started playing with me with a new set of questions...

But I was too tired after the practice session and workout, not to mention lack of sleep last night...

I shut down the app...

Put mobile on silent mode...

Dozed off.

Our first conversation

It was around 4:15pm when I woke up, but unlike the morning where I forgot everything about last night's fiasco… everything that happened from last night till the notification in the afternoon was keeping my head occupied, full of thoughts, questions, and a mild headache too…

I picked up my phone dialled the number of the canteen boy "Sanjay, one coffee aur marlboro advance ki dabbi le aaiyo saath vali dukaan se"

Five minutes passed.

Knock knock…

Sanjay entered the room with a cup of coffee and an advance box, I handed him 250rs for the cigarette packet, as he leaves. I followed him out of the room, adding to my headache the weather was hot and humid…

Coming back to the room I turned on the tv [to distract my mind from the questions regarding a girl whose name was the only information I had at that time and that too I got it a few hours ago from a profile on a social media site] before turning on the cooler I checked whether it had sufficient water in it or not and I found the water is enough for an hour or two so I turned on the cooler [every room consisted of a tv, cooler, two separate beds, two wardrobes and some rooms had ac but it was installed by the tenant and they had to pay extra charges for the electricity bill] a caretaker who plays the role of manager and a laundry guy too who stays at one of the rooms in the same PG...

I pulled out a cigarette from the packet, lit it up, and with the first puff that I inhaled it made me relax, after smoking two cigarettes consecutively and coffee with it while watching some old episodes of 'Tarak ehta ka ooltah chashmah', my mild headache decided to take a leave...

At that time, I was thinking why the fuck am I getting affected by an acceptance of a friend request by a girl. It's surely not the first time nor the last time that this happened...

I kept on watching 'tmkoc' for hours, but my mind was still occupied with some questions...

It was 7:00 pm when I turned off the television set as the repeat telecast was over... 'tmkoc' was that enjoyment factor of my life that occupied the space of my leisure and boring time...

'Sony sab' used to telecast old episodes of 'Tarak mehta ka ooltha chashmah' continuously for hours. To be precise from 1:00 pm to 6:30/7:00 pm every day and I used to watch it, so, I won't get bored or start thinking too much. But today it was different than usual, I was still occupied by some thoughts or I should say some questions...

An over thinker has some bad habits, they not only have questions in their mind, they try to even answer them or justify every possible option they have in mind not to others but to themselves only...

And I am an over thinker...

Question no. 1

Why did she accept my friend request?

She knows me?

If yes, how? I haven't seen her before or have I forgotten about it? No, she neither was my classmate nor schoolmate and I certainly did not share a tuition with her, nah my memory isn't that weak, no she doesnt know me.

[Contradicting your assumption is also a quality of an over thinker]

Question no.2

Has she heard about me in college?

Before we get deeper into this question there is a part or I should say part of my past you should know to understand this question [why this question]

Saloni Arora

A girl, which i got to know when i was in 12th standard, one of my friends made a bet against me that I can't charm her and the male ego of a teenager was hurt so, I started trying on her it took me three months but I was successful. The twist came when I got to know she had been diagnosed with cancer, I started getting emotionally connected to her, now my motive was to be with her so she can recover and be fine, but we lost that battle. It affected me, I got more hyper than before, lost friends, got myself into brutal fights, for a whole first year never went to college, used to leave house and went to a nearby gaming shop to play pool, and if you live in a small district, things spread very quickly and that's exactly what happened, I was being termed as mental and was a 'fun gossip topic' in college... there is more to it, but I think it would be enough for you all to understand question no. 2.

Has she heard about me? It's possible, I have seen her friend list and lots of people on that list don't like me or are the ones who think I am mental but then why would she accept my friend request.

No, it's not possible...

Question no. 3

Does she belive in having new friends?

Yes, yes this might be the reason. More number of friends makes the account look attractive and some genuine friends on that list are like icing on the cake...

After hours of analysis and a packet of cigarette II came to a conclusion; she is the kind of girl who likes to make new friends – jolly and fun-loving.

I decided, let's have dinner but still in my mind I wasn't sure, about my conclusion or her motive behind accepting my friend request....

After dinner, my daily routine was to either call or wait for my parents to call at 9, after having a conversation with them I picked up my bean bag and cigarette box and as usual, was sitting in the lobby…

Then I concluded and decided to ask her. Enough of hovering my mind around a simple question…

I picked up my phone and opened Facebook.

Opened Aarohi's profile.

Click on 'open chat head'.

And shut it…

It happened around thrice or four times before I was finally able to message her…

Dhruv: Hii…

And instantly a thought struck my mind if she wouldn't reply… and I was like "fuck Dhruv what the hell are you thinking and doing" you are not here for all this bullshit, you are here to achieve your dreams…

I pushed the lock button, shut my mind off as well. And start having my cigarettes and after some time, I decided it's time to sleep…

It was past 12[midnight] after settling into bed, I was about to doze off when a notification brought my phone back to life…

Aarohi: Hi

The sleep filled head of mine went on an overspeed ride, and i got conscious about how to plan this and work this out. Asking her with a straight face, why you accepted my friend request is not going to work here and it's a little awkward too… so...

Dhruv: How are you?

Aarohi: Fine

Dhruv: Hmm

Soye nahi

Aarohi: Bas sone lagi hu

Dhruv: Okay

And now I was like this is getting me nowhere, I want to talk a little more before asking the real question…

Dhruv: Aap 'Bihani Collegef' mein pdhte ho?

Aarohi: Haan

Dhruv: Dekha nahi kabhi college mein.

[I knew already what's gonna be her answer. Jab gaya hi nahi toh dekhonga kya ghanta]

Aarohi: Maine bhi tumko kabhi nahi dekha…

Dhruv: Haan ab main Gurgaon rehta hun isliye.

Aarohi: Okay

Then I decided it's enough I have to be courageous enough now to ask it. I can't take it anymore…

Dhruv: Dekha nahi, jante nahi toh request kyu accept ki…?

Aarohi: Jaante nhi toh tumne kyu bheji…?

And I was like "Damm yaar, bata na subha se soch mein pada hu…

Dhruv: Seeing 'Bihani College'in your 'about section' made me curious.

Aarohi: Ohh maine vaise hi karli accept, main karti nahi par tumhari vaise hi accept karli.

I won't lie I was smirking and thinking she is hiding something or maybe she is lying, but then I thought let it be…

Dhruv: Okay

Aarohi: Hmm

Chalo good night.

Dhruv: good night.

Our bonding

"Our bonding was not,

Perfect nor instant"

But imperfection has its own thrill.

And time has the ability to produce surprises, bring out different sides of yours and "comfort"

After our first conversation, I started being my normal self, the anxiety, the restless feeling was gone as I assumed she must have heard about me from her friends. Who knows me or was once my friend?

My routine was restored ... but

But something got added to that routine of mine...

The next morning, after sweating out in the academy and gym on a hot and humid day... as a daily routine of mine

I was watching 'tarak mehta ka ooltha chashmah' suddenly a thought struck my mind…

I picked up my phone…

Opened facebook messanger…

Dhruv: Hi

Sent to aarohi…

After some time, I received her reply, a formal conversation commenced again…

For a week or so, our conversation contained…

Hi, how's u, what's up, nothing much

And lots of "hmm"

Good night, soye nahi, bas sone laga/lagi hu...

But it ensured that we were on talking terms… then we started wishing each other "Good morning" … I started texting her more comfortably…

She was like a way to keep me connected to my college and city… slowly we started interacting about our mutuals, "How i knew them or how she is their friend, the hot topics of college, the incidences going on in the college, functions and many more…

Then our conversation and comfortable level reached to a point where we started asking each other "kesa raha din?"

Hate to admit it but I used to be a gossip guy with her… but I used to like it because at that time my only friends were my cricket buddy so, she was my closest buddy after cricket ground, I know this is not what we call "the closest buddy".

But to explain this is kind of tricky, so i will try… "She was the one with whom I used to talk and feel like I have found a person who looks after me in my bad times, happy times {a friend} whom I can talk when I am feeling alone or missing my parents, missing my hometown or my college [which I rarely did…]

Slowly I met new people, found some new friends and characters in my life… but friendship with her was starting to blossom day by day, I started sharing all things with her, it didn't matter how little it was…

One evening, she asked for my contact number… we exchanged our numbers or I should say when asked I gave her the number…

After a few minutes…

Mobile displayed

An unknown number

Calling…

Truecaller displayed

Aarohi

Rajasthan

I got anxious seeing her name…

Anxious for two reasons…

First, the girl I met or got to know about through a social networking site Facebook and the only information I had about her was that she was a senior of the same college [whom I had paid fees, to get admission and not even attended a single class] was calling…

Second before that day, for the last one and half years after the demise of Saloni, the female voices I heard were of either my family members or some kind of television/music star...

And all these thoughts and anxiety were on my face in just a few seconds or just a few rings of my mobile tune...

Accept decline

I received the call.

Aarohi: Hi

As soon as I heard her voice, I was awestruck, her voice was so beautiful and soothing to the ears...

The anxiety was less but talking to her for the first time was more challenging than I thought...

The conversation was formal and silence in between was the evidence of our awkwardness...

But hearing her soothing voice was something very relaxing, and hearing her voice I was not surprised because I got to know earlier that she won the best singer award at the fresher party during a conversation over Facebook chat...

The telephonic conversation was more like a silence competition. Who won, who lost is still a fact to discuss...

But after that conversation I was more comfortable with her, more relaxed. I started feeling, now I can share anything and everything with her without any hesitation...

The conversation from there on got personal too sometimes, informal, from chatting to a conversation over mobile calls [vocal]...

I shared my past or started sharing little things about my past or part of a past Saloni, about my family, a police case I got in, my anger issues, my fights, my ego and my likes and dislikes…

Seeing my comfort level, my comfortable approach towards her, or maybe something I don't know, that made her trust me more, she shared her past too…

Sahil

Her love once, when she used to study in Kota [Rajasthan], her family knew about them too… but the distance created a vacuum when she left Kota. And that was the main reason for their relationship to not work out the way she desired…

But in those conversations, I got my answer…

"Why did she accept

My friend request"

She said I saw your pic [profile picture] and I felt intrigued seeing your eyes [little wet]

"Bhai esa kya gam hai is bande ko"

Hearing this was a shocker, but later that day while smoking and enjoying my night routine, only one thought was going through my mind…

"Bhai esa kya gam hai is

Bande ko"

That was a time where my so-called friends left my side and here is a girl whom I haven't met before, a total stranger who understood my eyes and tried to know about me…

It made me happy, relaxed, and a little teary-eyed. All the happenings and mishaps in the last few years crossed my mind…

Then I realised, I have found a gem of a person as a friend…

I experienced lots of changes not only regarding her but at PG too… I found more friends, started drinking, and had some disagreements with her too…

I was a short-tempered guy and the most annoying thing for me was someone I care for, treat them as my priority saw my text and didn't reply. And one fine day, this incident happened between us…

I texted her later that evening, then after a few moments I saw a text containing seen notification at this particular time, I waited for some moments, but I was getting furious with every passing minute, so later in the night, I texted her…

"I don't like it if someone ignores my text and certainly not after leaving it on seen"

After some time…

Aarohi: Ignore nahi dhruv busy thi.

But I was furious

Dhruv: Koi itna busy nahi hota ki reply na de sake seen karke, sab bahane hai…

Aarohi: Dhruv esa nahi hota, insaan busy bhi hota hai…

This argument went on for a while, I was furious but one thing I was sure off that I didn't want to ruin my friendship with her…

So, I compromised my ego, my theories for her and it was the first time ever I did it...

Our conversation kept on increasing day by day; our bonding was stronger than before, not romantically but as a genuine friendship...

My friendship with other PG mates was getting stronger too... at the same time.

Sometimes i used to call her "babu" and vice versa but not in a romantic tone or feel but we were getting emotionally connected (I was for sure).

It was just another day of the conversation, and I was drinking at that time. after reading this she will be angry because she knew about my smoking but not drinking... after having a conversation and good night text I continued drinking till 1 after that I entered my room to have a sound sleep...

Speakerbox.... My phone tune annoyed me as soon as i fell on bed...

Aarohi...

calling

Accept decline

My head was dozing, making a circle as I entered the room, I took a look... it was some good hours between the good night text and the phone call...

I picked up the phone...

Hi, kya hua sab theek itni late call

Aarohi: kuch nahi babu bas neend nahi aa rahi thi

Hearing that babu at that time felt different and her voice felt different too either she was sleeping or upset about something...

The conversation was not about talking, it was all silence and some little whisper in between...

I don't know when we doze off without hanging up the phone...

The distance

"Distance is that part

Of any kind of relationship

That it either, tears apart

A relationship or makes it

Stronger"

So, our bond was getting stronger... my trust towards her was even more than before after that phone call... whenever I felt low, down, and out she was the one I came calling for [brightness in my life...]

We started sharing every little thing too, from emotional trauma to friends talk, to family issues to about my life in last year and a half...

Likes, dislikes for something or somebody, some late-night unexpected calls, little talks, chatting for whole day… our friendship was a happy, healthy, and a good one…

"When temptations are high

Destiny plays a trick in,

Both good and bad way…"

August

It was around "Rakshabandhan" when I received a call from my father in the afternoon, which was something unexpected and rare I picked up the call instantly he said he wants me to come home for "rakshabandhan…"

Temptation:-

It was more than a month that I haven't seen my family {especially my father}, I was and still, am far too emotional regarding my father, missing mother home-made food, missing duggu my pet. It is a pug

But on the same day I was suffering from high fever, later diagnosed as pneumonia… and to travel {a bus journey} at that temperature was a big roadblock for my temptation…

So, I politely denied…

But destiny had its tricks/plans… after disconnecting my father's call in a rather dull mood, a notification brought a smile to my face…

Messenger

Aarohi sent you a message…

Aarohi: hi

"After the disappointment

Of resisting the temptation

Of not going to home, her

Message was a shining light"

Dhruv: hi

Aarohi: Kaise ho

Dhruv: pneumonia

Aap kse ho?

Aarohi: haww, kse jarur kuch thanda khaya hoga, dhyan toh rakhna hai nahi...

After our formal conversation...

I told her about the conversation between me and papa...

Aarohi: toh aa jao

Dhruv: nahi yaar, mann to hai, par practice miss nahi karna chahta

Aarohi: are aa jao, family ko mile bhi toh time ho gaya...

"Then something struck my mind"

It's a good opportunity to meet her too...

Dhruv: chalo aata hu, aapko bhi mil longa

Aarohi: haan okay

I dialled my cousin brother [rahul's] number told him to book a ticket for Gurgaon to Ganganagar, then told Aarohi that I am coming...

Took some time off from her saying i have to pack my bags, then I went to have a shower packed my bags, informed my roommate about my home visit tonight...

Booked an ola auto... for Huda city metro station centre from my PG...

Boarded the metro... got off at Chandni Chowk... then from there, to a private bus stand on cycle rickshaw... boarded Vinod travels bus for Gurgaon to Ganganagar...

Reached Ganganagar at 4:30 am, and then due to tiredness I decided to have a nap till 8...

9 o clock turned the ignition on and excused my family saying I am going to college, but I was in no mood to mark my attendance at college...

Dialled a friend {Sidharth's} number... told him about my intentions, to have a drink at bar... he said Okay in an hour... I said done...

I had spare time in my hand I thought, why not have a smoke or two, at the nearest Dhaba to my college [our permanent place] for smoke and tea...

Texted her hii...

I didn't receive a reply.

After having a few smokes, dialled Sid's number, picked him up and went to the bar, and then a shocker, Sid has started drinking too...

When two friends, meet after a long time and especially over a drinking session, some secrets tend to come out, we started sharing our drinking incidences, happy, sad, and awkward too...

After our drinking session, we went home…

I didn't receive her message, and was constantly looking at her chat, checking whether internet connection was established or not…

The next day, I decided to go to college thinking if it was my lucky day, I might see her in college… but the day was unlucky…

I didn't receive her message the next day too… then I thought she might not be that comfortable to meet me…

"Rakshabandhan"

I booked the ticket for the same night…

The return route:

Chandni chowk metro station to Huda chowk to sector 12 PG no 1903.

After having an early breakfast, I went to sleep

Later that evening I received her message…

"For the first time, i was pissed off seeing her message…"

Dhruv: mil gaya time?

Aarohi: arre fever ho gaya tha, phir rakhi par time nahi mila…

But I wasn't impressed with this reason because I was angry that she didn't even respond to my texts, and moreover we didn't even meet…

And to be honest this created lots of doubts in my mind about our friendship… after that conversation, the vacuum in our trust and friendship was visible…

From long conversations to short conversations, and after a while no conversations…

Calls to no calls…

Slowly the distance was the only thing left in our friendship.

"distance"

My birthday

"Either distance creates

A hatred/agony or

Vacuum for love and care"

The distance from her didn't affect me a lot, but it did make a difference in my life… for a few days I was feeling amiss and it was noticeable in my behaviour towards others… she was one friend with whom I used to share everything…

But to be honest with you all, those two days when she didn't respond to my texts hurt my ego…

And, it wasn't that I had any kind of love feelings for her, but I was emotionally connected to her as I trusted her significantly… I didn't know why and when this distance created a situation without any disagreements, fights, or misunderstandings we just stopped interacting with each other…

But after a few days, the main purpose of my choosing Gurgaon [to pursue my career gave me a reality check…] and made me realise how distracted I have been for a few days… so after a few days, I picked myself up and started focusing on my sole love "cricket".

After a few days my routine was restored…

Wake up

Cricket

Workout

'Tmkoc'

Balcony time

Sleep

I won't lie I missed her…

Missed her most when I was out of form, family issues, not because I was in love with her, but because she was my solace…

Missed her when I achieved a target, scored heavy, or contributed to my team win because sharing these things with her used to give me different kinds of satisfaction…

August to November…

14th November 2015

As the time flew, I got back to my best being in terms of focus, the rigid behaviour, my focus was at its best, I got selected for club…

New friends, especially the guy name "Praful", well it's a story and some characters play a significant role as main characters…

Praful Bhaiya as I used to say

Used to reside two rooms behind in the same

PG, our friendship started from 2 cigarettes

{late night I was out of the stock of cigarette

And money... and I have seen that guy smoking before at late nights too so I knocked at the door

After seeing lights being on in his room}

Knock knock...

Hello sorry itni raat ko disturb karra hun, main Dhruv 109 no. Room, vo cigarette khatam ho gui hai aur maine aapko dekha hai kayi baar peete hue aur light jal rahi thi toh 1 ciggerete milegi, said all this awkwardly, meeting an unknown guy this late night, and that too just for a cigarette and that happened to be our first conversation.

Praful bhaiya: koi nahi, par superstar hai mere pass, he went inside his room picked up a small cigarette packet [gold flake superstar] it contained two sticks of cigarette...

Nahi nahi bhaiya 1 hi bahut hogi...

Are koi nhi lele, main to bas sone laga hu...

From thereon, we bonded well. One day asked him to pay online for a bus ticket, and paid him cash...

One day, I was having an evening nap somebody knocked at the door...

As soon as I opened the door Praful Bhaiya was the one who knocked at the door and till that time we become good friends, not best of buddies but a kind of sutta partner...

He said "bhai bahar jaana hai toh agar terko koi kaam na ho toh bike le jaaun, I said, haan bhaiya bilkul…

It was an early winter for me, being a guy who belongs to Rajasthan, late November is the time for winter to arrive, but it was just late October and I was feeling cold sitting outside my room which was my daily routine…

Late night, Praful Bhaiya entered the PG with one of his dearest friends "Kavish Bhaiya" and asked me piyega?

Kavish bhaiya was formally introduced to me by Praful bhaiya over a drinking session and a card game [teen patti…]

From there on "praful bhaiya" and "kavish bhaiya" were like my big brother and trustworthy people {a family outside the house}

14th November, (a day before my birthday)

I wasn't excited because I was away from home and secondly no one knew here about my birthday [I thought so] and then there were CA exams going on. Praful bhaiya and their group were busy with their examinations…

15th November (my birthday)

A chilly morning announced my birthday with lots of unexpected wishes.

I went for my cricket practice and received a surprise in the form of a cake and my face being the knife…

In the winter morning I had to wash up my face with cold water and this was anything but a pleasant surprise…

After practice, I went to PG, skipped workout that day, wore a blue denim, white t-shirt, and a black leather jacket…

Wishes were pouring over messages, whatsapp, calls throughout the day at regular intervals…

Surprise no. 2 came in the form of another cake, this time by CA aspirant circle of mine… after cutting the cake, ordered some food on Swiggy it was a small celebration as we all decided the 16th of November marks the conclusion of the CA examination and after that we will have a big party…

After a few hours…

My phone buzzed…

The display showed an unknown number.

I received the call

'Happy birthday…' a girl's voice shocked me… I checked the number once again

The voice was soothing to my ears…

Confused… I replied sorry who's this.

She "said guess?"

I got anxious because one of my friends or rather a girl with a big crush on me used to call me at unexpected hours and sometimes from unknown numbers…

I said "aayushi?"

She replied, "kon aayushi?".

I cursed myself for uninstalling the Truecaller app just two days before that phone call…

"Sorry yaar par awaaz se pehchan nahi paa raha"

"Aarohi" came the reply

As soon as the name with the soothing voice reached my ears i got awestruck... in my wildest of dreams I couldn't and didn't imagine to hear her voice again... and I am telling you the truth, it was over months ago and our conversation through any medium was zero...

"Happy birthday," aarohi said.

I was still awestruck but I regained or tried to regain my senses and said "thank you..." i said, "what a pleasant surprise" with a little bit of hidden sarcasm in the context of saying it...

Because when i started believing in our friendship she left me without any reason or prior notice... of her absence...

The conversation was very much similar to birthday calls...

Kse ho

What's up

Kya plan hai aaj ke

Same dull conversation and after a few minutes she said "chalo theek hai bye enjoy your day..."

I was smiling thinking she still remembers me...

And simultaneously, I was thinking now, how many days or months I have to wait again, to hear her soothing voice...

I celebrated my birthday with a few other PG mates, we decided to have dinner at the nearest hotel with drinks...

It was midnight, birthday was over but one last pleasant surprise was in store for me...

Our late-night conversation

"Long conversations feel nice

But

Late-night long conversations feel surreal"

It was midnight, I came back to PG, laid down on my bed, was smiling thinking about the whole day, thinking it was a great day [unexpectedly], took a look at the time, day was over, surprises are over I thought, time to have a sound sleep, skipped my smoking routine, as I was drunk and with drinks, your smoke count tends to increase a little more than usual...

But I was wrong [as usual] the surprises were not over yet... one last pleasant surprise was in store for me... [an unexpected phone call at an unexpected hour].

I was about to doze off when the usual culprit for my sleep-deprived nights came with a surprise this time... my phone started to make noise it was my ringtone… I picked up the phone… display showed "aarohi calling…", my blurry eyes were wide open now, I shook my head thinking I am seeing a dream, rubbed my eyes, and had a look at the display once again… it was indeed Aarohi written as the caller's name…

Aarohi calling…

Accept decline

I received the call

Aarohi: hi

I was shocked for two reasons…

1] I never expected to hear from her this soon…

2] It was midnight…

And happy… because I was talking to my long-lost friend… and her voice was so soothing to my ears…

With all those emotions and some alcohol inside my head… I came out of my room as I didn't wanted to disturb my roommate…

"Hi", I replied

Aarohi: kesa gaya birthday?

Dhruv: It was unexpectedly pleasant, celebrated with some PG friends, club friends, told her about the party plan of next day, told her about my new family away from home "Praful bhaiya" Kavish bhaiya" how our bond started over a cigarette and their exam [the added reason to celebrate my birthday next day again…]

Dhruv: aap kse ho…

Aarohi: main theek as usual…

"She used to say it every time,

Main theek hu as usual or

Main theek hu mujhe kya hona…"

I was smiling thinking how quickly I got back to my old self with her sharing everything and telling her every little detail…

We were having laugh, talking about the new people I met here, having some silly jokes… birthday party… and I took my opportunity to slip the question into the conversation which was hovering in my mind for the entire time…

"ek dum se gayab, bina bataye…

Aarohi: are yarr, ek ladki ki life mein kaafi issues hote, family problems, upar se study issues, friends sab khichdi ban gaya tha…

And I understood that because I know every girl has to fulfil some responsibilities…

I was humming a tune and a line from the song "wajah tum ho {hate story 3}" it was released recently… "main jo jee raha hu, wajah tum ho" as it was my new favourite song of that time…

Then I asker her "aapne suna…"

She replied, "nahi…"

"Sunna acha song hai" i said

"Okay abhi sunke aate" came her reply…

She put the call on hold…

And after a few minutes...

Aarohi: are tum itni feeling vala gaane bhi sunte ho... mjhe toh laga sirf rone vale gaane sunte ho...

Dhruv: arre mujhe ese hi slow and soothing songs pasand hai...

The conversation kept going on... suddenly a beep sound irritated me and the display showed my home screen... I opened the call log it showed last call 1 hr. 29 minutes 59 seconds so I knew we exceeded the time limit of a single call allowed...

She called back... I received the call on the first ring...

Aarohi: apne aap cut ho gaya tha pata nahi kse?

Dhruv: nahi, time limit complete ho gayi thi

Aarohi: esa bhi hota?

Dhruv: haan...

I was enjoying having a conversation with her... i got the feeling that I have found my long-lost ally again...

Memories...

Comfort level...

The conversation...

Everything was making me happy...

I watched the time and it was quite late and as I have to attend my practice session in the morning... so we decided it's time to conclude our phone call and conversation... as I should get some sleep before the practice session...

I disconnected the call... with a smile on my face, I surrendered myself on my bed and had a sound and satisfactory sleep...

It was short sleep, but a satisfactory one... I woke up as a part of my daily routine and enjoyed my practice session a little more than usual...

On my return trip from my club to PG, I stopped at the nearest recharge shop, decided to activate a "paisa per minute" facility as the last thing I want to come in between our conversation is hearing the "you don't have enough balance" message from a computer...

And, the silly thing about all these recharge things was that I did not even know when that kind of late conversation is gonna happen next between us... but i didn't wanted to take a chance...

Went for a workout.

Had lunch.

Our chatting routine resumed after what seemed like a long break...

After 6 in the evening, Praful bhaiya and the group arrived at PG with the happiness of, conclusion of exams message written all over their faces... and I was happy too for some obvious reasons...

We all outlined the party plan and the place was decided was our PG room {Praful bhaiya's room...}

Brought two liquor bottles from a shop {a scotch named Rockford reserve} of 650rs each... ordered some food online and some eatables from canteen and brought a new set of playing cards...

After a few drinks, we decided to play teen patti…

It was late but not midnight when I decided to pull out of the game due to a mild headache…

It was past midnight, I received a call and as expected it was Aarohi… I got up came outside the room for some privacy…

Neither did I tell her about the drinks nor my headache… as I wanted to have a conversation with her or I would say I did not want to miss out on an opportunity to hear her voice and laugh…

After the formal conversation…

Aarohi: kesi rahi party

It felt good as she remembered about what I told her, it always feels special when someone remembers the smallest of things too…

Dhruv: achi gayi, enjoy kara.

Aarohi: khatam ho gui?

Dhruv: haan [i lied]

Because I knew, if I would have said abhi nhi, she would insist me to join my friends and have fun…

The conversation started at the same time but lasted longer than the day before… after a few minutes, she said call karo… and I felt proud of my decision of having an active recharge plan in the morning…

Our conversation wasn't about a particular topic or point, it was diverse and pleasing, long but not dull {hmm, aur batao}, we didn't have to try hard to find a topic, we were happy with silly talks too...

From there on our conversations were frequent…

Sometimes long.

Sometimes short.

Late-night Chatting was constant.

I used to share lots of secrets with her…

She used to scold and advise me a lot…

I was enjoying her company… silly talks, my mistakes… it was going smoothly till… one night.

A conversation…

Communication of feelings

"Communication is a way to

Explain your feelings...

But some conversations

Brings out the emotions inside of you"

19th December 2015,

We created lots of memories over chats and interaction over the phone calls, but this date holds a special place inside my heart...

Our late-night conversations were frequent... and there were many changes in my routine, behaviour, it wasn't a tried one but it came unexpectedly and naturally...

I was less aggressive, I was trying to isolate myself from any kind of rift with her and anyone else which was very unlike me...

I started carrying my phone to the academy and I hate to admit it, but I used to practice with the phone being in my pocket...

I kept aside my ego {which I was proud of} only for her, I started texting her irrelevant of whether the last message was mine or hers...

Coming back to 12th December,

The day went as usual, but that day our chat was less due to some unknown reason to me... but my patience level toward her was better than initial days... and I must say, it was the most I got connected or was connected with any person at that time...

It was considerably late than her usual time for a call so, I thought she must be tired so, went to my room.... As I was about to doze off...

The room got lit up with the noise of the ringtone of my phone...

Aarohi

Calling...

Accept decline

I checked the time it was around 1... i got up quickly went out of the room without even wearing my slippers... soon I realised my mistake as it was freezing cold outside...

Received her call...

Aarohi: so gye the kya?

Dhruv: nahi, ek min hold karna, room se bahar aa jau...

Quickly went in, wore the sleepers, and picked my bean bag… silently shut the door [fog was all over the PG]

Dhruv: hnji…

Then began the conversation that I was not expecting… the conversation I wanted to avoid thinking she might be sleeping…

"a conversation that

Changed me"

Aarohi: kse ho?

As soon as I heard her voice, it felt she is sleeping or about to sleep or maybe just woke up in the middle of her sleep…

Dhruv: theek hu. Aap btao?

Aarohi: theek… as always…

Dhruv: soye nahi?

Aarohi: so hi rahi hu.

Dhruv: toh phir mujhse kon baat krra [smirking]

Aarohi: koi nahi, tum akele hi baat krre…

Now I was sure, she is asleep because of her voice and the replies that were unusual… I didn't lit up a cigarette, I thought the conversation might be small and she will fall asleep anytime sooner…

"Iwas wrong as usual"

It started as the funny conversation turned into a serious one… {pieces of advice were hurled over me… by her}

But in-between time to time, I kept asking her to sleep, saying you seemed tired, exhausted from daily work, you need some rest, it is late already, you need some sound sleep… but she was adamant, kept on denying, saying I am okay, agar tumko sona hai to so jao…

Then her go-to topic to scold me or advise me… Saloni entered our conversation and my afterlife… and I knew I was about to get a scolding or a piece of advice to move on…

Aarohi: tum bhul kyu nahi jate use, itna time ho gaya hai, move on kyu nahi krte…?

Dhruv: I tried, but the time, emotions, I invested in her was way more than I ever thought, tried to give her a few more explanations… but no use…

I kept on insisting her to sleep, and there was also a part of me that wanted to keep on interacting… her usual soothing voice was more attractive that night because of her low-pitched tone… whenever in between our conversations she said "Dhruv" it felt different that day…

During that conversation, I got to know that one of her cousins has arrived at her place in the morning, so, without asking I got the answer "aaj subha se chat kyu nhi ki"

But at all this time, I was feeling there is something different about her that day… it was not her voice only, it was how she was responding too… which was very unusual…

"and this time I was not

Wrong completely"

I had been a part of a long-distance relationship before, during one conversation I told her about that relationship, told her that "it is about the feelings rather than the physical touch, meeting regularly, dates, it is about the feeling of having them around..."

As the conversation progressed, the conversation took an intense turn, for the first time in all these months ... the conversation was not friendly, it was something different {intense}...

Aarohi: hug me

"speechless"

Dhruv: so jao aap abhi neend mein ho...

Aarohi: nahi krni toh manaa krdo

Dhruv: aisa nahi hai...

Before I could complete my sentence

Aarohi: toh karo...

And as I said before, I had been a part of a long-distance relationship before so I knew how to make this work, how to make people feel hugged...

Silence all around...

Aarohi: jo ladki tumhari life mein hogi, who bahut lucky hogi...

Dhruv: vo toh vo hi btayegi lucky ya unlucky...

I kept on insisting her to sleep... I was getting anxious... more importantly, I didn't wanted this conversation to move forward as I was still sure she is sleepy right now doing this interaction...

But she was more adamant than her usual self...

I was holding my guard, as I didn't wanted this thing to become something else and mess up our friendship the next morning…

The intensity of the conversation kept on increasing, and I let my guard down…

We felt hugged more and more…

Then the words i never expected to hear in my wildest of dreams, in my fantasy land too came straight out from her mouth…

"I love you"

A shiver ran through my spine.

I was speechless.

I was blank.

I was in utter shock.

Aarohi: kya hua?

Dhruv: samajh nahi aa raha kya bolu?

Aarohi: hmm… jo mann mein hai

Dhruv: abhi iska koi jawab nahi hao mere pass…. Maine socha hi nahi kabhi aisa… sorry…

Aarohi: koi nahi Dhruv, maine sirf apni feelings btayi…

Dhruv: hmm…

Still occupied with those words.

The conversation went silent…

We felt hugged more…

After a few minutes.

She hung up the call…

I kept on thinking about her and the conversation… lit up the last cigarette for the day… after an hour I dozed off…

Those three days

"Fear of losing loved ones hurts

But fear of losing a friend

Brings a different kind of

Emotion"

Those three days...

Before going to sleep... I turned off the alarm... for an hour after the phone call, I did not sleep... I didn't smoke as much as I do usually, when my mind is occupied with thoughts or some talks...

The conversation...

Questions...

Those three words...

And repercussions...

All these things kept my mind occupied added on to the conversation, lucky girl, move on, hug to "I love you…"

Question: She must be sleepy in an unconscious frame of mind, she might not remember anything the next morning, "what's next for us…

Those 3 words: "I love you"

Repercussion: If she wasn't in an unconscious frame of mind, what if my response to her communication of feeling hurts her, what if our friendship is the one that will suffer from this, what if…

"I lose her"

I woke up at 8 in the morning, feeling restless, with a grumpy mood… it wasn't my most peaceful sleep, my room partner was staring shocked at me… after I got up from bed, he asked, "are you alright…?".

I wasn't paying attention as I was desperately looking for my phone… my roommate again asked, "are you alright? I replied yeah, just a mild headache… ".

After searching the whole bed, I found my phone under the bed [switched off], my roommate went for a shower after looking at me doing all these things confused… completely ignoring his state I plugged in the charger… anxiously waited for my phone to switch on…

Anxiety of knowing whether she texted… {desprate I was…} but to add to my anxiety the result was negative…

Then, I looked at the time, and I thought it is too early, she might be sleeping or getting ready for college…

Then I looked at the notification panel, and missed call count asked for their due attention, 16 missed calls, I checked, it was from my club friends, I was about to dial one of the numbers, then a thought struck me, it will be a waste of a time to call them as I was sure they will be practicing now...

I took a shower, had my breakfast, decided to keep my workout session for the evening... kept looking at my phone for her text...

Sent a text

"Good morning"

Afternoon, I received my friend's call, "ae bsdk kaha hai aaj aaya kyu nahi practice par"

I replied bhai "kya hua aaj kuch jaruri tha kya itne missed calls... "

"Are tu roz aata hai toh socha bc utha na hoga utha dete hai, sab theek hai na ya raat ko jyada pee li thi..."

"Nahi bhaiya bas aaj neend hi nahi khuli..." I lied.

Toh gym aa raha na he asked i replied nahi [karan bhaiya, my cousin] ke ghar jaa raha unko koi kaam hai... i lied again...

"Okay chal kal milte phir...".

I kept on waiting for her text, staring at my phone displayfrom time to time, without hearing any notification sound...

Every time I heard a notification tone... my hope was, that it was from her but every time my hope and optimism wentin vain...

Morning too.

Afternoon too.

Evening

I cancelled my workout session for the day, my desperation level was getting higher with every passing hour, and with it my smoke counts were also increasing…

I tried, 'tmkoc', music, walking, cricketing drills, everything that distracts my mind from normal circumstances, but everything went in vain…

"Aarohi"

That day it was all about her, the questions were keeping my mind occupied…

Evening to

Night

No notification, no text, no calls… I kept on assuring myself… she might be busy… with this assurance I doze off, but not before deciding that I will attend my practice session as well as my workout…

Day 2

Woke up.

Practice session.

Workout.

Afternoon.

Received nothing from her side.

I was getting anxious, with every passing moment and it was hard for me to take this all alone…

"knock knock"

"Praful bhaiya kuch baat karni hai… sutta maarte hai aa jao…"

Praful bhaiya: "aaya"

After lighting up our respective cigarettes…

Praful bhaiya: "kya hua pareshan lag raha…"

Bhaiya ek friend hai... I didn't reveal her name I told bhaiya "bahut achi dost hai par parso raat kuch hua ab baat nahi ho rahi…"

Praful bhaiya: "abe pagal, ho sakta hai busy ho, jyada soch raha tu, jab keh raha hai achi dost hai toh jarur baat karegi…"

But that assurance was not enough to lift my mood…

The second day passed without her text and without knowing what is in store for us in the future…

Day 3

I was not at my usual best, and my friends noticed it… after the practice they asked me "kya hua be, ek din aaya nahi, aur last do din se khoya, khoya sa lag raha, phone baari baari dekh raha hai, koi panga hua kya, kisine kuch bola kya, bata bsdk ka naam abhi matter nipta dete hai…".

I laughed and said, " nahi bhai esa kuch nhi hai bas thoda sa fever ho raha", I didn't lie completely I was suffering from fever too…

It was the evening of the third day when I assumed my questions have been answered "I lost her"

After medicine, I was about to doze off, when my phone decided to ring.

Aarohi

Calling...

Accept decline

I quickly went outside the room and said...

"Kaha the?"

{without any hi, hows u}

Aarohi: "hein, ghar par"

Dhruv: "3 din se koi text nahi"

I was angry... not because of her, but because of the fear of losing her...

Jio communication was new in the market... and there were some technical issues with her sim due to which it got deactivated...

She told me about it, showed me a screenshot of text received from jio communication... stating your number has been disabled...

I retorted 3 din ho gye sahi hote hue... in an angry tone

Aarohi: haan kya ho gaya, itne hyper kyu ho rahe ho...

I was about to say ... but decided against it and decided not to talk about that conversation

I was my normal self after the initial burst of anger, I intentionally turned the conversation into another direction rather than telling her about these three days...

After the phone call... I was happy I didn't lose, my friend

As I thought about this, a tear rolled down from my eye.

"A happy tear"

Our first meeting

"First meeting always

Holds a special

Place"

12th December 2015

The first winter of Gurgaon, was too much to handle for me, I was diagnosed with pneumonia again and I was down with the latter one during that time…

Around 11, after skipping my practice I decided to skip my workout too, I received my father's call, he was worried about my health as I told my family about my high fever last night.

Papa: kesi hai tabiyat

Dhruv: pneumonia

Papa: ghar aaja

I was sceptical of this idea, as travelling late at night in this cold with this body temperature and that too a bus journey... I denied...

Papa replied, "chal dekhle, agr jyada tabiyat kharab ho toh aa jaiyo...".

It was afternoon... when a notification brought a smile to my dull face...

Aarohi sent you a message...

Aarohi: hi

Dhruv: hello

Aarohi: kesi hai tabiyat?

Dhruv: pneumonia

Aap kse ho?

Aarohi: theek hu

Tum apna dhyan nahi rakhte na.

As soon as she said thik hu... i knew there is something wrong... or else she would have replied thik hu, as usual, thik hu mujhe kya hona...

Dhruv: kya hua?

Aarohi: kuch nahi

Dhruv: pkaa?

Aarohi: haan

Dhruv: nahi kuch toh hai...

Aarohi: nahi toh...

Aarohi: kuch toh hai, bas bta nahi rhe

Aarohi: are, kuch nahi, bas friend ke kaarn pareshan hu…

Dhruv: kya kiya friend ne?

Aarohi: are meri ek friend hai Priyanka, usko jana hai Suratgarh aur mujhe saath chalne ko keh rahi hai…

Dhruv: toh problem kya hai?

Aarohi: bus pr jaana padega, aur mjhe bas ke dhakhe nahi khane…

I was about to send, koi nahi dost hai na… but, I erased all the text …

Dhruv: toh nahi jaoge bus mein…

Aarohi: par maan hi nahi rahi vo

Dhruv: koi nahi aap jaoge bhi, aur bus ke dhakhe nahi khane pdenge…

Aarohi: mtlb?

I was trying to create suspense…

Dhruv: main aa jata hu car pe le chalonga dono ko…

Aarohi: par pagal tumhari tabiyat kharab hai, aur aaoge kse gurgaon ho tum…

Dhruv: Dhruv, hu main aaj raat bus chadonga, subha vaha, itni tabiyat nahi kharab {I lied}

Aarohi: pagal mat bano.

Dhruv: are tum haan bolo bas, baki sab ho jayega, apne mil bhi lenge aur aapko bus ke dhakhe nahi khane pdenge {the main motive}

Aarohi: arre, dekhlo tabiyat na kharab ho jaye aur…

Dhruv: kuch nahi hoga, thodi der mein sab btata

Aarohi: okay

I dialled papa's number, asked him to book a ticket... he said kya hua abhi toh manaa kar raha tha, I lied, "college se phone aa gaya tha examination hall ticket ke liye registration karwana hai to aana pdega..." papa replied, "okay... karwake krta phone".

Notification beep...

Abhimanyu travels: your seat s2 has been booked from Delhi to Ganganagar...

Dhruv: final, kal aa raha hu main...

Aarohi: are, itni jaldi

I showed off a little, "dhruv hu mai".

After that, we decided from where I will pick her and her friend... I was excited... I started packing, told Praful bhaiya, about my visit to Ganganagar...

In all this excitement, I forgot my fever, it was around 7 I booked an auto, from Huda chowk to Chandni chowk metro, it was my preferred mode of transport, from there I checked into the bus...

For all the distance, the only thing I prayed was "no fog please", I don't want to reach late Ganganagar this time, as 8:00 was the decided time to pick her and her friend...

Fortunately, the bus reached Ganganagar at time... picked up two dairy milk silk from a variety store near the bus stand...

At 7:45, I picked up my car and left for the college [the information I provided the family...] I picked her friend from Rashtriya school, near my house... and then stood waiting for Aarohi outside octave showroom in block area around 400m away from her home...

I wore a white t-shirt, blue denim, and a black leather jacket...

Then a girl with a height of 5ft 5 inches, wearing denims, heels, and a yellow fluffy jacket whom I knew as Aarohi was approaching the car...

I unlocked the car, she entered, and said, "jaldi chalo jaldi chalo..." i started moving the car, she was hiding herself behind the car seat by bending down on seats as our route to Suratgarh, we had to go through the street that leads to her house...

After crossing some distance, she got comfortable, her open hair, childlike laugh, and a smile that can hypnotise anybody was mesmerising me...

Then she said, "yeh kya gaane chala rakhe hai, mujhe do aux..."

And it's an hour trip to Suratgarh from Ganganagar and for 2 hours {including return trip} we heard just one song "Main rahoon ya na rahoon" ft Emraan hashmi...

We didn't talk a lot during the drive...

After reaching, Suratgarh, as I stepped out of the car, she said "tum to chotu se hu..."

We laughed...

Then, I got to know, her friend's purpose of visiting Suratgarh was to meet her another friend and I was frustrated thinking I have come here travelling 400 kms for this but then I felt relieved as the thought passed my mind if I haven't been there what would have Aarohi done alone...

We left her friend and that guy at the mall and went to a nearby park as she likes to play with small kids, we didn't talk much, just kept looking at each other from time to time...

After a few hours, we came back to mall, had our lunch... together 'our first meal together'.

The mall was relatively new, less crowded, so we decided to take a walk around mall...

Then the conversation took a turn.

She said "phone pur hug krte ho ya sach mein bhi itni achi karte hoo..."

I blushed... yes, i blushed...

We tried to hug in one of the corners of mall... but it was small as we heard someone footsteps...

We didn't talk much...

Her friend said, "okay chalte hai". I said okay, me and Aarohi walked towards the parking...

We got into the car, and that time we hugged tightly, and this time without any fear, she kissed my forehead...

Then her friend came and we were enroute to Ganganagar... this time she was sitting in the front seat... after a few kms she put her head on my shoulder

My favourite memory.

I dropped her near her house… her friend, near the same place from where I picked her up…

And went home…

Our first meeting.

Our first meal together.

Our first hug.

My favourite memory…

Misunderstanding

"People say ego destroys

a relationship

I say misunderstanding

which are created

destroy relationships"

On Christmas eve, I boarded a bus for Gurgaon and on the return trip I was listening to my new fav song, "itna tumhe" by Yaseer desai... thinking about her and her memories, texted her to inform her about my departure from Ganganagar...

You all will be thinking, I travelled hundreds of kms and only one story related to that visit... nah there are many and they all deserve there different mentions...

There was something in that visit that changed me, I returned to Gurgaon as a different Dhruv… a noticeable change was in my temper issue as it was milder than before… I left some of my temper back at Ganganagar it seemed like that to my friends…

I reached Gurgaon on Christmas, we wished each other we were talking happily … she told me “we will celebrate this new year together” and as usual, I was happy hearing that…

But things started to turn different from there on…

I felt something different in her behaviour, but she was adamant saying nothing… I thought it might be some family issues… and she is not comfortable in sharing all these, so after her persistently denying about it, stopped asking her about it…

The conversations started drying up…

On the new year eve… we had a chat, I told her I will call you at 12 she replied “no, i will tell you when to make a call…”. I agreed.

But after the new year our conversations were either little or none… I asked her she said, my sister is at home so, I can’t talk much I was fine with it because the thing with me at that time was I must know the reason, I can’t just wait sitting for my people and don’t know the reason for their absence…

During that period, we had some arguments too, to be precise two arguments…

First argument

I was out to buy a cigarette packet, so I decided to lit a cigarette, as soon as I lit up a cigarette…

The phone rang and displayed Aarohi.

I picked up the phone.

I was happy to hear her voice.

After having a formal interaction.

Aarohi: Tumne Sidharth ko kya btaya hai?

Dhruv: mtlb?

Sidharth was our mutual friend… my buddy from standard 6th and her family friend…

Aarohi: Sidharth ko kab btaya apne baare mein aur kya?

Dhruv: Apne movie dekhne gaye the tab vo apne saath hi tha na, aur yehi ki dost hai kyu? Kya hua?

Aarohi: pakka?

Dhruv: haan kya hua?

Aarohi: kuch nahi bas ese hi

Dhruv: okay {in angry tone}

Aarohi: chalo talk to you later

Dhruv: see ya.

I wasn't happy with the way she talked, but I knew there is something, that she is hiding

Second Argument

It had been some days, we haven't had a conversation and it frustrated me… I picked up my phone

Texted her… kuch issue hai ya problem toh bolo na

Aarohi: I will call you in some minutes

In our conversation… I was angry and she was cold-hearted.

I asked her, "kisi ne college mein mere baare mein bola kya…"

First, she denied then… she admitted and accepted, "mere friends khte hai kis pagal saath baat karri hai"

I laughed… "aap mujhse baat krte ho pagal lagta hu kya?"

Aarohi: nahi

Dhruv: toh

Aarohi: par

Dhruv: par?

Aarohi: mujhe tumse darr lagta hai

Dhruv: what, come again

Aarohi: mjhe tumse darr lagta hai

Dhruv: toh mat kro baat, bye

And without listening to her, I threw my phone away literally…

Adding to it I made a grave mistake…

It was the month of feb 2016,

I was excited and upset both at the same time.

Upset: I was living with a lie that stood in front of me that day… and I thought how big of a fool I am [but this incidence doesn't affect the story of Dhruv and Aarohi so not a detailed version]

Excited: I just scored my highest run for the club...

I was drunk... and with all these things in my mind and in that drunken state, I forgot to look at the time and dialled her number... but it went unanswered.

The very next day I received her text... stating because of you, my mom scolded me...

I said sorry, and told her everything that had transpired...

Her response was cold...

So, I knew she was angry... I said, sorry again, I will not call or text you first from now on...I promise, you won't get in trouble again because of me...

All these things crept into our friendship and slowly we were again on the downward spiral...

But this time I didn't gave up.

It was the Valentine week, so I decided it's better to resolve all this, meet her and clear everything in person...

I went to Ganganagar... waited for her to come out of college, because I felt the best time to have a conversation with her was while I was dropping her at home...

But for the first time she denied for it, on the second day Sid was with me, so Aarohi and Priyanka both agreed, and at that time I was listening to 'kinna sohna' from Johnny Gaddar on the loop.

So, she asked me about the song and that was the only substantial talk we had on that Ganganagar trip of mine...

I felt disappointed and left for Gurgaon the same night… Slowly I started thinking, I am losing her again…When I saw her this time she seemed more beautiful…

In March 2016, me and Praful Bhaiya decided to watch "Fitoor" late-night show… I was affected visibly and Praful bhaiya wanted to distract me…

I was about to enter the cinema hall…

My phone buzzed…

"Dhruv tumse ek jaruri baat karni hai", texted Aarohi.

Now you all must be thinking about why I was so affected?

This is the answer.

New year

After Christmas, our conversations were neither frequent nor heart-warming...

"Realisation is a kind

Of confusion, it takes time

But then you realise, hint

is always there..."

For the first time, the lack of conversation with her didn't affect me, my mind was occupied with the thoughts of her, she wasn't physically present near me, but in my mind, it was all her, her child-like laugh, her smile, her untied hair, her eyes, her smile that can brighten anybody's dull mood...

From 25th December to 30th December 2015.

I was happy, I was in good form, therefore I wasn't losing my temperament that quickly.

I kept on thinking about her, our meetings, the touch we shared, the little things which I never classified as romantic before, but with her it felt surreal…

It might be my superstition, but whenever i had someone who genuinely cares or loves me, I always score more…

On the 30th night, I thought why am I getting so obsessed with her, what the hell is wrong with me… but when you are an overthinker, you analyse everything…

So, I picked up my cigarette box, bean bag settled myself on the balcony, and started analysing…

My analysis:

She cares for me.

I have a great bond with her.

Meeting her felt different.

And then my heart said:

"Shut up"

And accept that you have fallen in love with her.

With a smile, I thought the hint was always present, my concern towards her, never wanting to lose her… waiting for her texts, changes in routine… keeping my ego aside for her…

But I am dumb, I realised this late…

All those dumb thoughts while analysing this were making me laugh…

I thought, I may have fallen for her even before she communicated her feelings... so, I decided that on New year's, 1st of Jan, 2016 is "the day..."on which I will convey my feelings...

On 31st December, we had a chat, I told her that, "I will call you at 12 but she disagreed and told me "I will call you when I am free..." I agreed.

We decided [my CA aspirants] friends that we will celebrate the eve on one of the vacant flats of Kavish bhaiya...

At 7 we started the arrangements for the party...

Wines, rum, raw chicken, marinated chicken, hookah, cigarettes...

The guest list was bigger than I predicted

Kavish bhaiya

Praful bhaiya

Gaurav bhaiya

Ashish bhaiya

Rajan bhaiya

Sukhi bhaiya

And kavish bhaiya's younger brother and his friends...

Around 9, we started the party, I was enjoying it but my focus was on my mobile, I wanted her to call so, I can express my feelings...

Drinks started

Smoke...

Chicken {half burnt}

Cards

Countdown

It was 12 we wished each other… I texted her "happy new year" drinks were on refill mode… I was in the middle of a drink when I received her call… I went outside in a small balcony adjoining the flat and staircase…

Dhruv: happy new year

Aarohi: happy new year

She told me when we were chatting that she will call around 2 but it was hardly 1 so,

Dhruv: apne toh late kaha tha

Aarohi: jaldi time mil gaya

Dhruv: mjhe kuch kehna hai

Aarohi: bolo

Anxious or what we say now, butterflies in the stomach kind of situation I was in I took a deep breath.

Dhruv: yr, kse kahu, I realised something.

Aarohi: kya

Dhruv: "i love you"

Aarohi: okay

Dhruv: okay

I thought, my response when she communicated her feelings at that time, is the reason behind this 'okay' only… so, I didn't react, I decided to give her time… After a few minutes.

Aarohi: kya kr rhe the?

Dhruv: pee raha tha…

Aarohi: mat peeyo, promise karo ab nahi peeyonga…

Dhruv: I promise… {without hesitation}

The call ended on a happy note I thought.

I didn't drink, after that the half-filled glass that I left on the table when the call arrived went undisturbed for the rest of the party…

I was a hookah lover…

So, after that call, I smoked hookah only, till I got a headache… I slept around four.

Near 7, Praful bhaiya woke me up and we went to our PG…

So, now you all know why I was so affected by that misunderstanding…

Patch up

"Getting back something/someone

From the verge of losing is

Satisfaction"

I was waiting outside the PVR for another show to conclude when my mobile vibrated inside my pocket…

For the last few days, I lost hope of seeing her message and notification stating Aarohi, so annoyed because of the disturbance, I said "kon hai bc is time…".

But to my surprise, notification displayed:

Aarohi sent you a message…

Aarohi: dhruv car chahiye thi…

Confused I said, "okay, kab?".

Aarohi: kal

Dhruv: kal toh possible nahi hai, main Gurgaon hu… prso de sakta…

Aarohi: parso toh viva hai uske agle din?

Dhruv: haan koi issue nahi…

Aarohi: haan dost saath jana hai puchke btati hu…

These words felt like a knife pierced through my heart… dost saath jana hai kyu aur kon?

Dhruv: okay bta dena

Aarohi: okay… good night

Dhruv: good night

I started feeling heavy, the conversation left me distorted… and to add to this miserable state of mine, konsa dost or kyu jana hai inko uske saath… this "fitoor" movie gave me a headache…

We came back to the PG… hurling abuses at the movie and the person who recommended us this movie… but I was angry and disoriented more because of the conversation that transpired just before this movie and the way it went…

But I promised her…

Later during the movie, I received her text, "Friday ko possible hai kya?", and to that i replied "I promise mil jayegi". {big mouth i am}

The next morning, I dialled my cousin's number for ticket booking…

And as every trip to Ganganagar theroute was the same, from Huda city centre to Chandni chowk… but I was in for a surprise today. The buses [every private bus} from Delhi has been deemed cancelled due to a protest at JNU, I called my cousin, told him to ask about the bus situation for tomorrow…

I was angry because I did not want to let her down, wanted to fulfil the promise I made, I came back to the PG fuming and smoking cigarettes continuously…

I decided to book a cab rather than metro just so that I could smoke … as I reached PG, Praful bhaiya asked "kya hua vapis…?" I let out my frustration, narrating the incident with abuses as a grammar… and helping verbs.

He laughed… seeing him laugh and already venting out my frustration and realising its Tuesday and I have some time to fulfil my promise I smiled a little and after some time dozed off without knowing…

The very next morning there would be a bigger shock and surprise in store for me…

My phone woke me up with a call from my father,

Papa: tera aana jaruri hai kya?

Dhruv: ram, ram papa hnji internal exam hai

Papa: aayega kse?

Dhruv: bus se papa kya hua, jnu vaala khtm nahi hua kya?

Papa: nahi, jaat andolan

Dhruv: hnji?

Papa: news dekh

I turned on the tv, headlines stated jaat andolan for reservation has been commenced from today onwards…

Papa: buses aa nahi rahi college mein baat krle phir bta

Dhruv: hnji

I was frustrated, and angry emotions were getting the better of me…

I started smoking, thinking about her, my promise, I picked up the phone and dialled papa's number, said "jaipur aa jata hu vaha se chacha ticket krwa denge…"

Papa: jaipur kse aayega?

Dhruv: papa roadways chal rahi hai pata kar liya… [i lied ki pata kar liya hai but actually chal rahi thi]

Papa: jaruri hai toh aaja vrna rehne de risk nahi lena…

Dhruv: jaruri hai papa tabhi aa raha hun.

Papa: okay…

I dialled one of my local friend's numbers, told him about my situation, and asked him to get ready, we are taking your car to Jaipur… he was one of my closest, so he agreed.

We met after an hour and a half, we started our journey, crossing distance safely but near Dharudhera, border of Haryana Rajasthan… a small group of people waved at us to stop…

With the language we were sure that we are in trouble as they are jaat…

They told us to go back, my friend was Haryanvi himself, he replied to them politely and told them a fabricated story… but they were adamant…

Half an hour passed…

I was getting frustrated, I signalled something to my friend and he instantly knew I was about to do something foolish and we are in danger...

Those jaat were talking standing near the driver seat door with us through window, I gently opened the door lock and threw the man away with the help of the car'sdoor and accelerated the car...

Fortunately, they were a group of 5-6 people only at that time... then a thud sound made both of us afraid ... a brick came shattering the rear mirror inside the car...

I pushed the accelerator a little more...

Till Jaipur, we were silent, looking around and backward from time to time to check if someone was following us?

As we reached Jaipur, first thing we looked for was a Honda showroom to replace the shattered mirror and I asked him to take some other route back the next day...

He laughed and knowing I can reach Ganganagar before Friday I afforded a smile too...

I went to my Chacha's flat, the ticket was booked and the boarding bus was from Jaipur to Ganganagar made me relax... but soon after the question, 'konsa dost, kaha aur kyu came knocking...'

But then I thought let it be, I have made a promise to her, and seeing her smile is all that I wanted because that smile brightens my life... I will be able to fulfil my promise...

Thursday...

As usual, I was at the Dhaba near my college campus, smoking during college hours waiting outside for her with the reason of dropping her home so I can see her smile... but she denied and it did make me furious... I accelerated the car way back to home...

Evening

Aarohi sent you a message...

Aarohi: dhruv kal pkaa ho jayegi na car?

Dhruv: konsi chahiye?

[At that time, we had an i20, dezire, and an Innova]

Aarohi: Innova chahiye...

5-6 jane hai...

Dhruv: Okay no issues

I was happy seeing that text, "okay". Her group was going for a trip as its their last year in college.

Aarohi: dusri cars toh dosto pass bhi hai par koi adjustment nahi ho rahi thi toh merko yaad aaya tumhare pass innova hai...

Dhruv: haan koi issue nhi hai kal de donga...

Next morning

I went to Sid's house. His and Aarohi's house were around 500 m apart... I told him the whole scenario.

Sid: tu bhi jaa raha hai?

Dhruv: nahi

Sid: chutiya hai kya bsdk gaadi de raha, ek toh terse pucha nahi upr se gaadi de raha ek ldki ke bharose...

Dhruv: are dost hai theek hai na...

Sid was about to reply when Shubham one of our school friends and her friend arrived at Sid's house...

Shubham asked, "Sid ki bhai Aarohi ne car ka kaha tha... he knew everything but Sid acted like he knew nothing... nahi toh.

I was quietly watching all this sitting in the car signalled them and told, "merse hui thi baat le jaa car..."

They took my car dropped me at Dhaba, I told Sid, he said he will be there in an hour and a few minutes later i saw them crossing the Dhaba, Aarohi was sitting in the middle row of the driver's side seat...

After an hour, I and Sid went to watch the movie 'Neerja...'.

At 5 in the evening, they came back Shubham and one of the other guys came to the destined place to give me back my car keys...

In evening,

Aarohi: Thank you so soo much because of you humari ek all-time memory create ho gui.

Dhruv: anything for you.

Aarohi: thank you.

Dhruv: arre thanks mat bolo

But the conversation was not heart-warming...

A few days later, there was an annual function... I went to Sid's house normally... not for the annual function.

Sid: Aarohi varo ko chorne jaana hai aur vo keh rahi hai Dhruv ko mat laana, toh car de main chor kr aata hu...

I felt hurt, that day I was furious and when the function concluded, I said with a straight face "main utar jaata hu Sid chor aayega..."

Aarohi: kyu, peeche adjust ho gaye hai hum...

The night before farewell... there was a gap of one day between the annual function and farewell.

Aarohi: kal farewell hai.

Dhruv: [I was still hurt] best of luck.

Aarohi: tum aaoge?

Dhruv: nahi.

Aarohi: kyu?

Dhruv: main kya karonga?

Aarohi: jo sab karenge.

Her asking about me after so many days made me melt...

Dhruv: aap chaloge saath?

Aarohi: nahi jaongi toh cousin ke saath {rohan}. Par aaongi tumhare saath pakka...

Farewell day...

I wore a red coloured Nehru jacket, a white shirt, and black trousers... she wore a black and pink saree... during farewell it was an overall boring day, I remember a funny incident...

There was a spoon and lemon race. As soon as it commenced I told Sid, Aarohi nahi jeetegi isse hansi to control nahi hoti, and that's what exactly happened.

During the final hour of farewell Rohan approached me and said "bhai merko kaam hai toh meri cousin hai use drop kar dega?", Rohan was my classmate during school time and he didn't know that I and Aarohi knew each other well…

So, I said, "haan bhai koi nahi".

Aarohi and Priyanka came…

Aarohi: ache dikhte ho formals mein, pehna karo…

Dhruv: (blushing) okay.

Aarohi: abhi ghar nahi jaana…

I was more than happy to oblige… I turned the car on a long route, things started clearing up… "Sid was the one who said Dhruv is mad, drink karta hai, bhadkaya usne hi tha" she said…

I was furious but more excited about the prospect of finding my lost friendship with her…

I asked aapko kya lagta hai… she said Sid galat tha sry and thanks ab yeh mat puchna yeh thanks kyu…

For the first time, I went to her home to drop her off… gave her one of my caps which I decided last night as a present for her farewell … later she sent a pic with a photo signalling an 'A' from her hands, I got her back from the jaws of no hope…

Memories

Long drive.

On the day of our first meeting, in the evening we decided to meet the next day for a long drive...

Aarohi: ab main tumko forehead kiss nahi dongi.

Dhruv: kyu?

Aarohi: maine aaj kiya... tumne nhi ki isliye...

Dhruv: {blushing} are main drra tha kya sochoge aap.

Aarohi: ab main karne bhi nhi dongi.

Dhruv: ese kse ab toh mera darr nikal gya.

Aarohi: no.

Dhruv: dekhte hai.

The next day I left home a little early, picked her up from the same spot as the last day... she told me the time when she wants to reach college... after a little calculation I decided 30km distance and return would be enough and perfect...

I tried my best to be as slow as I could be... she put her head on my shoulder {every time she does that my heart skips a beat} I kissed her on her hair, she shook her head signalingI was no...

I kissed her hair again, this time she held his face up... a kind of gesture that made me realise it's not an opportunity it's her way of saying yes... and I kissed her on the forehead...

So, I won my challenge with her help...

From Lalgarh, I took a turn, as we approached the college 100 m before the campus gate, my car got stuck in a hole... I asked her to go attend her class, I will manage, with some help I was able to pull my car out and left for Sid's house...

A day in college

For the first time in 2 years, I went to college and stayed inside the campus for more than an hour...

She told me or I would say instructed me a day before, "you are coming to the college campus and i don't want to listen to any excuse...".

I wore a blue denim and a white-red hoody...

I was standing near the accountant's office... when I saw her approaching... she was with her friend... she stopsped near me and her friend went into the girl's locker room...

She took out a paper and a pen and asked for an autograph... I was shocked then I realised during a conversation I promised her my first autograph will be for you only...

I signed that paper... after college I dropped her off near her home...

Movie

I decided to leave for Gurgaon but when I informed her, she said not yet and I was so influenced by her that I cancelled the booked ticket just two hours before the bus timing...

She planned for a movie together the next morning, she still is a Deepika Padukonel denied fan, and at that time 'Bajirao Mastani' was doing great at the box office...

I told Sid about our plan as her friend Priyanka was supposed to join us, Sid said main aur Priyanka 'Dilwale' dekh lenge which got released along with 'Bajirao Mastani.

So I went with Aarohi for 'Bajirao Mastani...' as soon as 'Deepika padukone' made an entry, Aarohi screamed, the only one in the whole PVR cinema... then she put her head on my shoulder and we held each other's hands and then I entwined my little finger with hers as we kept on watching the screen...

A few minutes from intermission she got scared as her family called and asked her about her whereabouts... during intermission she felt relaxed when she got to knew it was just a normal query due to some household work...

After intermission got over, she stopped me near the gate and waited for everybody to leave that passage. She gave me a tight hug… kissed each other on the forehead before getting to our seats…

We weren't able to watch the climax as her family was calling her to come home early and I promised her I will watch the climax with you only…

A day after patch up

I woke up in the morning with fresh energy as I had Aarohi back in my life also with the lots of notifications on Instagram.

Aarohi tagged you in a post.

It was a collage picture consisting of all her friends with names given by her.

Mine was a caring friend…

A shocker.

During my trip to Ganganagar in March {patch up} I noticed a thing that she had a bandage on her left hand, I asked her twice about it, at first she told me that she got injured during some household work…

But after patch up and my 2nd year exam conclusion I went to Gurgaon and one night she told me the truth.

She injured her hand in anger over a boy named Shubham… it hurted me, so I drank that night after the New Year's Eve.

But I didn't react as I thought the vacuum that misunderstanding left was filled by him… so I accepted her decision and respected that…

An exam

It was during my 2nd year final exams. One of our exams was scheduled on the same day, I was happy for that exam.

I picked her up from the decided 'pick up point' and we went for the exam together.

And my luck on that day was quite good, as her roll numberand mine was in the same classroom, therefore I was distracted throughout the whole exam and I kept looking at her after every 10 minutes.

I left the hall 30 mins earlier, she came and said "itni jldi bade tez ho… ". She asked me that some of her friends need a lift to sangria and I happily obliged as for me it meant more time with her.

She asked for my phone's passcode, I obliged and she saw my cigarette pic and she was furious I. lied it's an old pic…

A trip to Suratgarh again…

It was during my 2nd year exam, Aarohi called and said Suratgarh jaana hai aaj dopahar mein… I excused myself from home saying, "I have a tuition in the afternoon".

I was late due to some family reason A,arohi was waiting for me near the college campus. On reaching there, I got to know that Priyanka had some kind of an exam in an hour, I accelerated the car and was about to reach Ganganagar in around 40 minutes.

Priyanka said I forgot my wallet back at the place where they were waiting for me which had her Admit card…

So, we were in a situation in which we couldn't get back home before the time we told our families and she was in no position to give her exam. That day we spent the most time in each other company thanks to Priyanka...

November 15th, 2016

On the 22nd of October, I was upset due to some family issues and I told Aarohi about it but after that she called me on my birthday and told me she is getting married...

I went numb for days...

On the 20th I saw her social media post stating 'I said yes'.

It shocked me.

After a few days I went berserk, we had an argument, I was angry and I said a lot but later I realised her Naani was no more... and it broke my heart, I let my anger on her on the same day when she lost her precious family member.

The next day I wrote a sorry letter and told her I will be there for you and I respect your decision just be happy...

Jan 2017, I texted her but didn't receive a reply till morning.

6th Feb 2017, I was on a road trip to Ganganagar, I received lots of messages where she stated that her marriage had been cancelled, her fianc e was a mad possessive guy with drinking issues...

It felt like destiny had some more tricks for us...

A conversation

It was November 2017, I was at Salasar that night...

During our conversation she asked, "kitna pyaar karte ho...?"

Dhruv: saari khushuyan dene ka waada nahi karta hu par aansu nhi girne donga iska waada karta hu…

The next morning, she replied: hupp.

A silly talk…

One night I told her that a cat was crying in the wake for her lost children.

She said, "yeh itne bache kyu karte hai?".

I laughed

Aarohi: yeh kr kse lete hai itne?

Dhruv: jse aap hoye the…

Aarohi: vo to papa mummy so nahi paye jaldi…

I laughed at this hard so many times after…

15th November, 2017

I wanted this to be my favourite memory, but I never knew it would be my last with her.

It was the 14th night and I was excited to see her wish me first.

At 12:10, I thought she might be tired and sleeping right now.

At 9:00 am wishes from friends and family started pouring, my eyes were just waiting for that one notification.

Aarohi sent you a message.

Morning passed.

Afternoon passed.

With every passing minute my hope for this happiness was fading away,

No party from a party freak this time, no excitement or cakes or beer.

11:59, video call from Aarohi

Aarohi: Happy birthday.

Dhruv: Thank you [face down]

Aarohi: lookup, I know you are sad but I forgot the date and when realised I wanted to be the last one to wish you... and now lookup.

Dhruv: no, why would be i sad, you wished me, and it's more than enough for me [with moist eyes and a tear rolling down]

After the video call I received a text.

Aarohi: tum mere liye kya ho main janti hu aur main tumhare liye kya hu vo bhi.

Don't be sad.

Bolne se bass darti hu.

20th feb

"Every story has an end,

And sometimes its unexpected"

It's been 18 days and we haven't had a conversation with each other after an argument...

2nd Feb 2018, I was back at Ganganagar and joined the family business after my final year exam... it's been months leaving Gurgaon and she was the only shining light left after I left cricket...

I was frustrated the way things were going [family issues], no friends, and to add on to it she wasn't talking to me for months properly [after November, 2017]

On the 1st of Feb, I texted her "yaar mjhe ek side krdo, clear krdo kya hai yeh sab beech meihn latka kar rakha hai, baat krte nhi online reh kar bhi"

Aarohi: kal call par baat karte hai.

Dhruv: nahi, main aapki awaaz sunke shaant ho jaata hu.

Aarohi: kal call par pakka.

Dhruv: nahi abhi.

Aarohi: abhi mjhe neend aa rahi hai.

Dhruv: {furious reading this} Okay.

The next morning, 2nd Feb

I lied to my family that I have some important work regarding my mark sheets at college, I wanted no interference and disturbance in our interaction…

I was about to start my car when my phone started making a noise.

It was Aarohi.

I picked up the call, accelerated the car and was a few metres away from home when our conversation began.

Aarohi: haan ab bolo.

Dhruv: baat karte nhi online hokar bhi. kya chal raha hai kuch toh clear karo, beech mein latka rakha hai mjhe…

Aarohi: I have started working as a teacher in pre-nursery school and aur or bhi kaam hote hai.

Dhruv: toh yr mera kya? pata hai na kesi situation mein hu upar se aap baat nahi krte…

Aarohi: roz baat karna jaruri nhi hota Dhruv.

Dhruv: par kabhi toh kro yr, clear krdo aaj kya hai apna.

Aarohi: Dhruv main to hamesha dosti rakhongi aage tumhari mrzi…

I was hurt, this was not the answer I wanted or expected.

Dhruv: Okay ab jab aapka msg aayega tbhi baat krenge…

I never knew it would be our last conversation for 18 days. We didn't know what we were up to. No talks, no posts no chats…

19th Feb, I was feeling restless during the night time and was thinking what could be the reason?

It was past midnight on the 20th Feb.

That night I was scrolling through the news feed on Facebook again…

Aarohi:

I am very lucky to have found you and to spend the rest of my life…

Aarohi got engaged to Sanket.

And I was shell shocked for hours, I kept looking at the post and the pictures… I didn't know when sleep took over, when I woke up, I opened Facebook, searched Aarohi and hoped to not see that post again and to believe it was just a nightmare but I saw that post again…

The whole day I was feeling numb and restless. After every 15 minutes, I was leaving the shop for cigarettes nothing pacified my feelings, not the sleep nor the cigarettes that day…

My friends who knew about Aarohi were calling me… "I am okay", was my automated reply…

During that time I used to work out at home... but that day I didn't work out I was dull, numb, restless, wasn't able to understand my feelings...

What struck me...

At 9 in the evening, an hour earlier than my usual time to shut my room, I excused myself from my family saying "sone jaa raha hu..."

I went to the balcony adjoining my room...

Opened Facebook.

Searched Aarohi.

Clicked on the post.

Saw her comments.

Started smoking.

Memories were flashing inside my head...

I was writing all the memories, the days into the Notes app.

The anxiety, the restless feeling from the morning turned into tears, cries and screams till I fell unconscious on the balcony...

A story that started three years ago, on a balcony with a Facebook profile...

Ended on a balcony with a Facebook post...

"Arz kiya hai, har nasha azmaya maine,

Par uske saath rehne ki alag hi talab hai"

Thanking note

Thanks to all the people, who stood by me during this whole time, parents for being so supportive...

Especially,

Remandroom- a group of brothers that guided me during my writing and helped me at every stage of this book... from cover to the last page.

Thank you so much...

Printed by Libri Plureos GmbH in Hamburg,
Germany

9 789356 115309